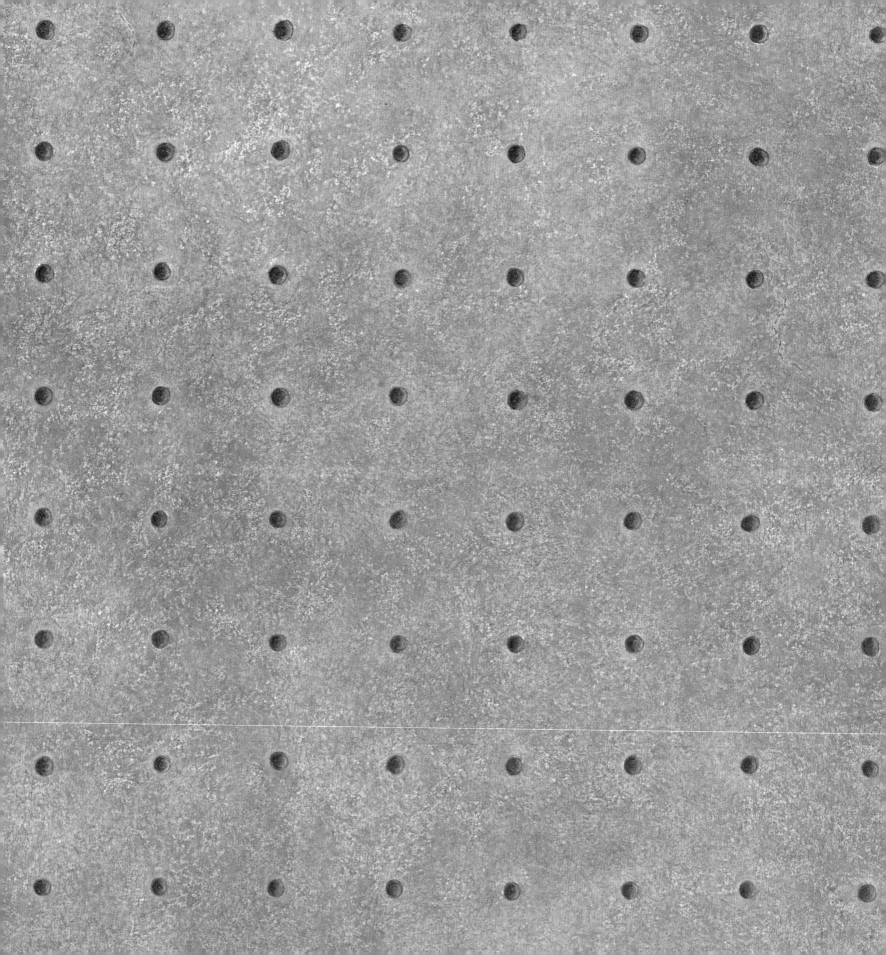

CHINESE FABLES

"The Dragon Slayer" and
Other Timeless Tales of Wisdom

Shiho S. Nunes

Illustrated by
Lak-Khee Tay-Audouard

TUTTLE Publishing

Tokyo | Rutland, Vermont | Singapore

CONTENTS

Acknowledgments

I thank my family and friends for their help and encouragement in bringing this collection of stories to publication: Wallace W. Allen, Lizabeth G. Ball, Susan Miho Nunes, Gerald and Pauline Gifford, Jean S. Matsumura, Richard Sisler, and David Swartz.

—Shiho S. Nunes

To Father, omniscient and omnipresent, for whom nothjing is impossible.

—Lak-Khee Tay-Audouard

Preface

Who doesn't remember "The Tortoise and the Hare" or "The Lion and the Mouse" or "Belling the Cat," and recall the lessons these simple stories teach? Fables are among the stories we hear first and remember longest.

If you went to Sunday school, you will have heard the "Parable of the Server" and the "Parable of the Talents." A parable, like the fable, conveys some truth or moral lesson, but it does so indirectly by using a comparison of some kind. The New Testament of the Bible teaches many lessons through the use of such comparisons.

Wherever they came from, whatever their source—Greek, Hindu, European, Asian—these tales, with their moral teachings and ageless wisdom, are an important part of our literary heritage.

In China, cautionary tales, like fables and parables, have a long and illustrious history. They are part of a class of works called *yu-yen*, writings with an underlying—a second—meaning. Yu-yen also include allegories, metaphors and anecdotes. These works are very old. China's golden age of fable was in the fourth and third centuries BCE, but some yu-yen go back even further. The more recent ones were written between 1644 and 1911. These writings were not accessible, however, until Chinese and European scholars and folklorists collected, translated and published them in modern form.

From three such collections Wolfram Eberhard, an American folklorist, abstracted and cataloged five hundred tales in his *Chinese Fables and Parables*, a monograph on Asian folklore and social life. The cataloged entries are brief, giving only the story line in two or three sentences, rarely more. An unmistakable thread of humor runs through many of them. Devoid of detail, the entries cry for invention.

And invent I did with the nineteen entries I selected to expand into stories. I have taken liberties, I'm sure, but tried to remain true to each story's original intent as nearly as I could interpret it. As fables and parables the world over have always done, these Chinese tales illustrate both the wisdom and foolishness of ordinary folk.

The Practical Bride

A bride was being borne in a sedan chair from her father's house to her bridegroom's home in the next village. Four porters in jackets of identical color and design carried the gaily decorated chair. Small bells tied to the corners of the canopy kept merry time with the porters' gait as they jogged along. The tapestry hangings over the canopy roof and sides concealed the passenger within, but everyone knew that a bride was being taken to her new home. The villagers stood outside their doors, waving and calling out well-wishes and farewells as the chair passed by.

Midway to the next village, a loud rrriiippp!!! interrupted the merry tinkling of the bells. CRASH! THUD! The chair fell to the road, taking with it the silken cushion and the bride, and leaving the porters holding a pair of poles with an empty canopy and dangling shreds of rotten rope. The bride picked herself up carefully. Not a single ornament of her elaborate headdress was out of place. She moved to the side of the road to await repairs. But no repairs began, only a chorus of complaints and blame.

"Did you check the chair before we started?"

"Nobody told me to!"

"It was bound to break! See how cheaply it's put together!"

"Master should have bought a better chair!"

"And he should have sent two chairs as a precaution!"

"Well, what can we do? We have no tools; we have no cord."

"You run and tell Master to send another chair. We'll wait here."

"But it will be dark by the time I get back!"

"And if it rains, where can we go for shelter?"

"Oh! What's to be done!?"

Out of patience, the bride took charge. She stepped between the poles where the chair had been and ordered the porters to take their places. "Start jogging!" she said firmly. Hidden under the canopy hangings, she kept pace with them. The bells resumed their merry tinkling.

In this fashion the bride jogged to her new home, arriving in state and on time, with every hair ornament in place, and none of the guests the wiser.

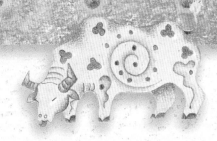

The Wrong Audience

Kung-Ming I was an accomplished musician on the ch'in, the seven-string zither, the Chinese scholar's instrument. Excellent though he was, he had one great failing: he didn't care a snapped string about his audience and paid no attention to the response of the audience who came to hear him play.

Kung-Ming had studied the instrument in the old-school belief that it is the way to purity and harmony with the universe. To Kung-Ming playing the ch'in was meditation: he withdrew into himself, thought only lofty thoughts, and cared nothing about the effects of his music on his listeners. To enhance his purity, he often played the ch'in in a secluded pavilion or on the banks of an icy mountain stream. He best liked playing alone under a full moon on a hillside overlooking the town.

One day Kung-Ming came upon a meadow bright with sunshine and wildflowers and a brown cow grazing on clover. The scene was so sunny and peaceful that Kung-Ming was moved to bring out his ch'in, to celebrate the meadow, the sun, the brown cow. He plucked from the strings a run of sound so joyous it made his own heart sing.

The sun shone on, the meadow bloomed, the cow grazed on and did not even lift his head.

Slightly annoyed, Kung-Ming produced a series of trills and ripples like the warbling of songbirds and the burbling of brooks, sounds so beautiful he felt himself almost melt away to become one with the meadow, the hillside, the brook, the brown cow.

The sun shone on, the brook burbled on, and the brown cow continued grazing, though she twitched an ear and flicked her tail at the flies on her back.

Thoroughly annoyed, Kung-Ming struck two loud, discordant notes—Twannnggg!! Zzzinnnggg!!

"Mooooo!" lowed the cow, lifting her head to look mournfully at Kung-Ming before going back to munching grass.

"Verily I have the wrong audience," said Kung-Ming to himself. He left the meadow a wiser musician, with an awakened appreciation of those who came to hear his music.

11

Stealing the Bell

When finally the city fell to its besiegers, the great House of Fan was vacated and left to looters. Master and servants packed what they could carry, buried the gold and fled.

Then the mobs came. Ordinarily law-abiding, the townsmen turned into rampaging hordes that emptied the abandoned mansion of everything: carved tables and chairs, inlaid screens and chests, rich carpets and tapestries, priceless garments, porcelains and ivories, every wok and kettle in the kitchens.

An outburst of plunder and looting seized the city until a proclamation from the new authorities halted the frenzy. Infractions, however minor, would be punishable by death. Quiet settled on the city.

Among the servants of the House of Fan was one Ch'in, a poor man always at the bottom of the domestic scale. He did not flee the city with his master but sneaked away to join the pillaging mobs. He saw a chance to start his fortune.

When Ch'in returned to the House of Fan, he saw the front gate fallen, the doors pried open, the house emptied. Nothing of value remained. But in a disused storeroom behind the empty tool house, Ch'in found to his joy a large bronze bell. It was so big his arms could barely encircle it, and it was too heavy for him to carry.

Poor Ch'in was torn with indecision. Here was the only thing of value left in the great House of Fan. Should he abandon it? Of course not—he had found it! Should he ask his wife's brothers to help him? But they were a greedy lot, sure to demand more than their fair share. Should he borrow a cart? But this would mean traveling the streets, and discovery would mean death.

A brilliant thought slowly lit up his eyes. He would break up the bell into several pieces that could be secretly carried away piece by piece. Its value as a bell would be lost, but there would be the value of the metal. Of course!

Ch'in returned to the House late that afternoon with a sledgehammer he had taken from one of his wife's brothers, and a bundle of rags for wrapping the pieces of bronze. Eagerly he set about his task of breaking up the bell.

BBBOOONNNGGGGG!!!!!

The first strike was so loud Ch'in nearly jumped out of his skin. He dropped the sledgehammer and wrapped his arms around the bell to silence it. "This will never do!" he thought. People will hear the bell and I will be discovered. He looked about frantically for something to muffle the sound. His eyes fell on the bundle of rags he had brought. Hastily ripping one into pieces, he stuffed up his ears. For good measure he tied a strip around his head to keep the plugs in place.

Ch'in resumed breaking up the bell, confident the noise was now too muted to be heard beyond the walls.

Sakyamuni and Lao-Tse

A painted statue of Sakyamuni sat next to a statue of Lao-Tse on a shelf in a humble mountain temple off the beaten track. As you know, Sakyamuni is one of the several names of Buddha, the founder of Buddhism. And Lao-Tse is the philosopher who founded the way of life called Taoism. Whoever first placed the two statues side by side must not have cared that they should be sitting together on the same shelf. Thus the two sat in intimate comradeship and exchanged many a quiet observation on life and religion and the travelers who stopped at the shrine.

"A life of the utmost simplicity and naturalness is our universal ideal," Lao-Tse might murmur. "To follow the Tao is to follow the path of life that leads to self-realization. Is this so different from the Buddhist ideal?"

"Life is full of suffering," Sakyamuni might reply. "And suffering can only be ended by enlightenment. One path to enlightenment is to shed earthly desire, and one way to shed earthly desire is to return to a simple life. So really," Sakyamuni might conclude, "we are not far apart on our basic rules for living."

Thus they quietly conversed, never raising their voices, for they sat side by side.

One day a Buddhist monk strayed from the beaten path and stopped at the small shrine. He frowned to see Sakyamuni and Lao-Tse sharing the same shelf. With a firm hand he moved Sakyamuni to a higher shelf before he began his prayers.

Not long after, a Taoist monk discovered the shrine. Shaking his head in disapproval, he grasped Sakyamuni unceremoniously by the shoulder and lowered him to his former position on the lower shelf. He then carefully elevated Lao-Tse to the upper shelf.

From that time on, the shifting of Sakyamuni and Lao-Tse up and down continued. Travelers who found the shrine moved the statues according to their religious beliefs. There was no peace or rest for the two, and now they had to shout to each other to be heard. Conversations became exhausting.

"Ah me!" Lao-Tse lamented loudly. "See how dirty we've become from all the handling! And how unsettled we are. To think that once we sat peacefully together."

"Ah yes!" Sakyamuni yelled from the upper shelf. "Stupidity has destroyed our peace."

The Same Sickness

Chang was a retired merchant, not immensely rich, not miserably poor, just somewhere in between. He was eager to provide tangible evidence of his status in the scheme of things, so he filled his house with furniture and bric-a-brac he bought at sales and auctions at prices that pleased his merchant's soul.

His latest treasure was a handsome bedstead decorated with carved ivory and mother-of-pearl inlay. Chang could not wait to show it off. Imagine his disappointment when the bed would not fit into his crowded parlor! Reluctantly, Chang had it placed in his sleeping chamber, at the back of his house.

Whenever visitors were expected, he climbed into bed—a sick man propped up against his new bedstead. Of course, there was always an opportunity to point out the perfections of the ivory and mother-of-pearl inlay. But word spread that Chang was ill and dying, and a stream of visitors gave him almost more occasion than he could handle to show off his treasure. He almost never got out of bed.

One day Chou, the father-in-law of Chang's oldest daughter, traveled from the city to see him. Now, Chou was a modest man, but he did have one vanity: he loved gay, multi-colored socks and loved even more to display them. He always wore his trousers high to expose a bit of color beneath the cuffs; and when he sat, he hitched them up—not so much to prevent bagging at the knees but to show his socks to best advantage.

"Well, In-Law," said Chou as he sat down beside Chang's bed, arranging the knees of his pants, "for a sick man you look mighty good—bright eyes, lots of color, no lost flesh. What ails you? What does the doctor say?"

"I really don't know." Chang tried to look as sick as possible. "I have good days and bad days."

Chou's attention had wandered a bit, for he suddenly remarked, "Hmmm—a new bed."

Chang sat up, visibly brightened, and threw back his covers. "Never mind the state of my health, Chou," he pronounced. "I'll live. Look, I want to show you my new bed!" He threw aside the pillows to reveal the panel of ivory and mother-of-pearl inlay. "Look at that workmanship! Isn't it superb?"

Chou burst into laughter and swung his gaily-colored stocking feet onto the bed. "You know, In-Law," he gasped, "I think you and I have the same sickness!"

鄭樂琪曰壹壹

Everybody's Talking About It!

Mao K'ung loved gossip. He loved even better the art of embroidering the stories he heard. Nothing gave him greater pleasure than to add a fancy stitch or two to give a story color and novelty for the entertainment of his friends and family. He was a very successful embroiderer until he came up against the sage Ai-tse.

"What's the news from home?" asked Ai-tse one day. The question was the perfect opening for Mao K'ung's specialty.

"Oh!" Mao exclaimed, clasping his hands in wonderment. "Everybody's talking about it. A farmer in Chi-mo has a hen that hatched a hundred chicks!"

"Nonsense!" scoffed Ai-tse. "Impossible!"

"Well, maybe there were two hens," Mao conceded, recognizing that his stitch had been too extravagant.

"Still impossible!"

"Then maybe three, or five—a couple more?"

The sage was impatient. "Why do you keep increasing the hens instead of reducing the chicks to a number that can be believed?"

"Because *I* prefer increasing the old instead of the young," Mao mumbled, crestfallen that his story had not impressed the sage.

Ai-tse laughed. "Well, what else is happening at home?"

Mao's face brightened. "A miracle!" he cried. "Just the other day, a whole side of beef fell from the clouds on to South Road, enough to feed the village."

"From the clouds? No!"

"It must have been. The meat just appeared. Nobody put it there."

"It could have fallen from the butcher's cart."

"The slaughterhouse is on North Road," Mao insisted. "The butcher doesn't travel on South Road!"

Ai-tse grew impatient. "Let me ask you, Mao, where exactly on South Road did the meat fall down? If you can tell me that, I'll believe your story."

In earnest Mao protested. "It must be true because everybody's talking about it!"

The Vigilant Sentry

Li Shih-min was locked in a great power struggle with his brothers. To spare his people the horrors of war, he took his army far afield and set up camp on a plain. At night great watchfires were lit, sentries were posted, and everyone was alerted for an attack that could come at any time.

Early one morning as Li was leaving camp with a small guard to check the outposts, a sentry stepped into his path and halted him.

"Sir!" the sentry cried out, saluting. "Do not leave camp today!"

"And why not?" Li asked, half angry at the man's boldness but impressed by his earnestness.

"I had a terrible dream last night," the sentry answered.

"Oh?" Li said. "And what was this dream?"

"I dreamed you were ambushed near the river. The attackers were too many and could not be repulsed. Much blood was shed."

"I thank you for the warning," said Li, and he gave the sentry ten taels of silver before he signaled to his men and rode away.

That evening the sentry was relieved of watch duty and assigned to the daytime chore of scouring pots. He was left to wonder why he was rewarded with silver in the morning and demoted that night.

Kwan—yin, the Goddess of Mercy

There was once a farmer who worked hard, saved his money, and gave something to his temple every feast day. Sadly, however, he was not a filial son. He was ashamed of his mother, who was wrinkled, threadbare, and simple with age. He saw in her what he would someday become, and he feared and hated it. And so he was not kind. He spoke harshly when he spoke to her at all, had her eat meals alone, and sent her to her room whenever visitors called. His mother endured his treatment with never a word of complaint.

Now most of the villagers, faithful Buddhists all, wished to make a pilgrimage at least once in their lives to the shrine on Put'oshan to Kwan-yin, the goddess of Mercy. Her statue was said to shine with the true spirit of mercy and would richly reward those who made the pilgrimage.

And so one autumn day, the farmer set out for the shrine. After a journey of many days he reached P'ut'oshan and followed the crowds to the little temple. Imagine his disappointment to find that all the statues there were dingy and dusty, worn down by the finger marks of countless worshippers.

The farmer complained to an old woman who stood outside the temple.

"Everybody told me there was a true Kwan-yin here, shining with mercy. But where is she?"

"Oh, it's not easy to recognize her," the old woman said, "not unless you have mercy in your heart. She always wears an old robe of hempen cloth wrong side out and shoes the wrong way. But most people who believe in her are able to see her."

Disappointed and puzzling all the way, the farmer walked slowly home. After several days he reached his gate as the sun was setting and found his mother bent over her broom, sweeping the path to the house. She opened the gate to him with a shy word of welcome. With new eyes, the farmer saw that she was dressed in her old hempen robe, wrong side out, and wore her shoes the wrong way.

The King of Beasts

One day a hungry lion caught a fox and was about to devour him. "How dare you eat me!" the fox demanded from under the lion's claws.

Astounded, the lion loosened his hold. "What?" he growled.

"Don't you know that _I_ am the King of All Animals sent here by the gods?" the fox said. "They will punish you if you eat my sacred flesh!"

"They will?" The lion loosened his hold a bit.

"Of course!" the fox warned. "You are my subject, as are all the animals in the forest, big and small."

"Prove it!" cried the lion. Hunger gnawed at his sides, but he was a cautious creature. Slowly he lifted his paw.

The fox wormed his way out from under the lion's claws. "Follow me," he ordered. "Every animal will run away in terror when they see me coming. And well they might!"

The two set off, the fox proudly ahead, snout regally high and tail aloft, the lion slinking behind him like a servant in tow. And just as the fox had predicted, every animal they saw scurried off into the bushes as the two approached.

"See," said the fox, and he dashed off into the trees and disappeared, leaving the lion hungrier than ever—but, hopefully, a little wiser.

A Small Gift

A poor country boy came to the city to see the famous teacher, Kung-San Lung. Bowing low before the learned man, the boy said, "Let me study at your feet and learn to become wise like you."

Kung-San Lung was pleased that a simple country boy had traveled so far to become his pupil. "What abilities do you have?" he asked kindly.

"Abilities?" The boy was puzzled.

"Yes, skills, attributes, accomplishments—anything you do well, anything outstanding."

The boy answered without hesitation. "I have nothing except a very loud voice."

When Kung-San Lung introduced the boy as a pupil to the other pupils, they all laughed. They made fun of his country ways, his lack of city refinements, his loud voice. The boy said little and kept to himself.

One day Kung-San Lung took his students into the mountains to gather specimens of the plants they were studying. In their zeal the boys scattered far and wide over the mountainside, and when the time came to start home, four of them were missing.

Cries and calls went up from many throats.

"Loo!!"

"Ying!!"

"Where are you?"

"Han!!"

"Chan!!"

"Come back!"

The trees absorbed the cries; no answers followed.

Kung-San Lung beckoned the country boy to his side and led him to a rocky outcrop at the edge of the valley. "Let us see what your voice can do," he said.

The boy climbed up the rock, braced himself, and lifted his head.

"Ying!"

"Loo!"

"Chan!"

"Han!"

"We are here!"

His voice blasted forth over the mountainside like a trumpet, a bull horn, a thunderclap. It stilled the birdsong, shook the pine needles, bounced off the crags, and rolled down into the valley.

Once more it resounded.

"Ying!"

"Loo!"

"Chan!"

"Han!"

"We are here!"

It was not long before the missing boys emerged from the trees.

Kung-San Lung turned to his students and said, "Even a small gift has its uses."

Cooking the Duck

Two brothers went hunting on an early autumn day. The weather was turning cold, and they waited a miserably long time before a flock of wild ducks appeared low in the sky. Excited and expectant, they hunkered down into the reeds at the margin of the pond to watch the approach of the birds.

"I can't wait for Old Mother to fry the duck!" said the first brother eagerly. "I can just taste it!" He smacked his lips.

"Savory duck with chestnuts is better," the second brother countered. "You can't beat that."

"Duck fried in peanut oil," the first brother insisted. "Crispy in part, tender throughout. That's the only way to cook duck!"

"The only way?" the other protested. "What about savory duck with eggs? Or with bamboo shoots and black mushrooms? Now, there's a dish fit for emperors!"

"Fried duck, with a touch of ginger, garlic, and scallions. That's the way we're cooking this duck!" the first brother shouted, and he aimed a blow at the other's head.

The second brother caught the raised fist and kicked at the other's shin.

Alarmed by the shouting and tangle of flailing arms and kicking legs, the ducks flew away.

What's In a Name?

Younger Brother was given a cat he named "Tiger Cat" because her fur was striped like a tiger's. He felt hurt and angry when Big Brother called her "Cat."

"Cat, here's some milk," Big Brother would say, or "Cat, go outside."

When Younger Brother protested, Big Brother only laughed.

One day Younger Brother's friends came over to see his new cat. "This is Tiger Cat," Younger Brother said proudly, holding her up for all to admire.

"That name's too common," one boy said. "Call him 'Dragon Cat' instead!—dragons are lots stronger than tigers!"

"No!" another boy broke in. "Dragons need the clouds to hold them up. 'Cloud Cat' is a better name."

"Then 'Wind Cat' is even better!" insisted a third boy. "A strong wind can blow away any cloud!"

The fourth boy cried out, "A wall can stop the wind! I say 'Wall Cat'!"

" 'Mouse Cat'!" the smallest boy piped in. "A mouse can destroy the wall that can stop the wind that can blow away the clouds that can bear up the dragon! So mouse wins!—he's the strongest!"

Big Brother had been listening. "A mouse can be killed by a cat, you know," he broke in. "So are you going to name her 'Cat Cat'?" He looked over at Younger Brother. "What's wrong with just calling her 'Cat' and being done with it? Does she really need a title?"

And bending down, he called, "Here, Cat," and with a loud meow, she came running.

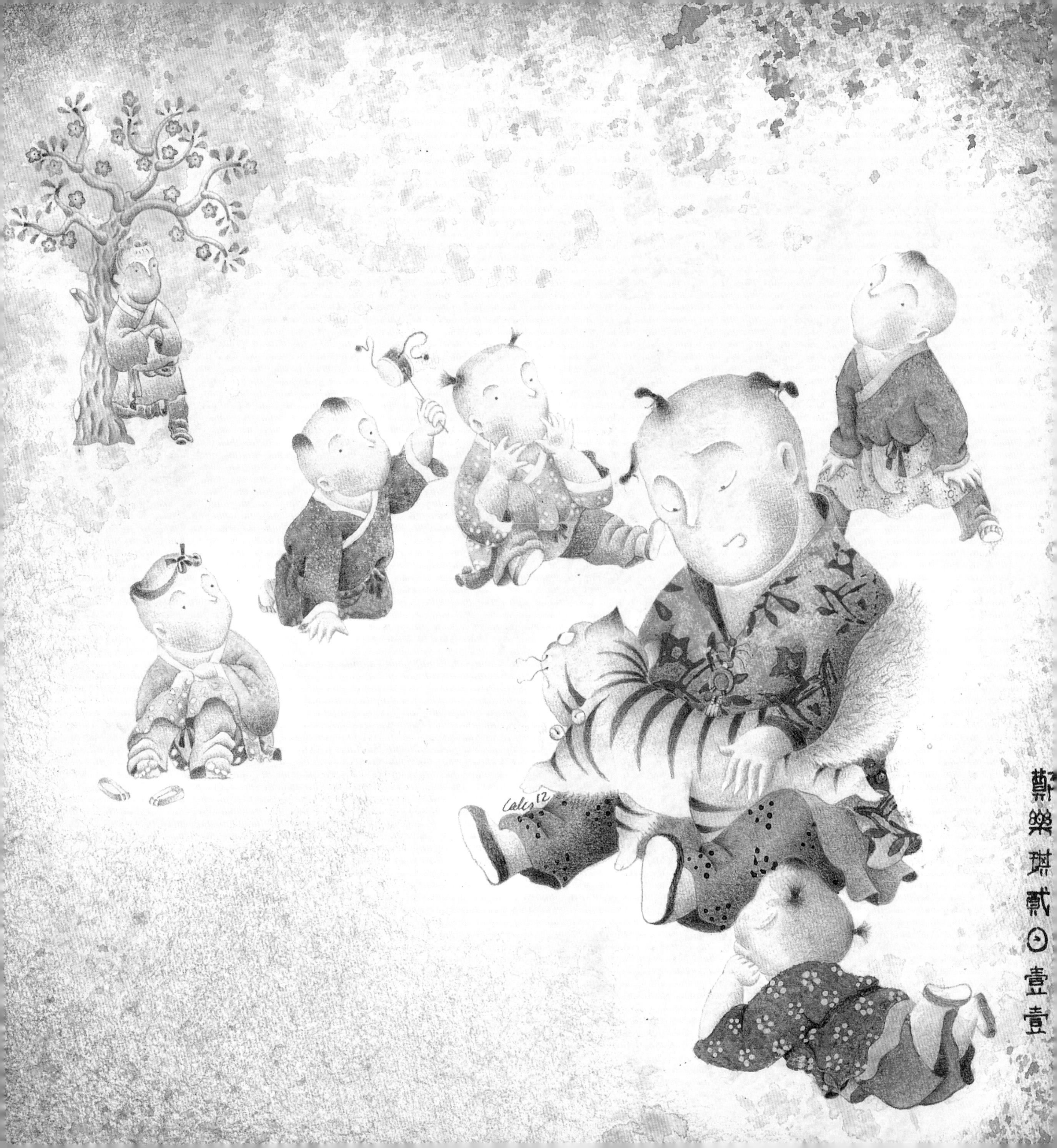
鄭樂琪貳〇壹壹

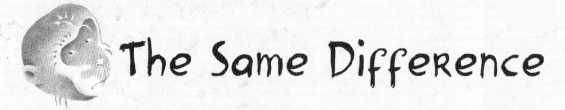# The Same Difference

An old man kept a dozen monkeys and took loving care of them. He gave them the run of his cottage. He fed them before he ate his meager meals and gave them whatever tidbits and sweetmeats happened his way. He talked to them endlessly as though they were his children and was sure they understood him as well as he understood their monkey chatter and monkey ways.

There came a time when a great famine descended on the land. It followed a long drought that withered the fields, and a heavy flood that washed away what remained. The old man was left with little to eat, but what remained he shared with his monkeys.

One day, when his store of food was almost gone, and he knew that what remained would have to be severely rationed, he said to his monkeys, "I will give you three taro in the morning and four in the evening." He signed the numbers with his fingers as he spoke. "Will that do?"

The monkey faces fell, the mouths pulled down, the chattering stopped. All twelve looked woefully at the old man.

Cut to the quick, the old man thought for a moment. "All right, then," he said. "I'll give you four taro in the morning"—and here he counted out four on his fingers—"and in the evening I'll give you three." He folded down a finger. "Now, isn't that better?"

The monkey faces brightened, and an excited, happy chattering filled the cottage. Thus the problem was settled to the satisfaction of the old man and his monkey children.

44

Scaring the Tigers

Two monks were returning from their annual fund-raising journey through the mountain villages and towns served by their temple. The money and pledges they had collected was almost enough to pay for the maintenance of the temple and the keep of the priests and acolytes for another year. This year the requests for donations had been greater than usual because the temple bell had cracked and would have to be replaced.

Their path wound through a bamboo forest. The older monk, a seasoned veteran of fund drives, kept a sharp lookout for tigers, a known hazard in these hills. The younger monk, a hairless stripling, was completely oblivious to danger. He was carrying the heavy subscription lists and totally absorbed in adding up the numbers.

"Seventy-five!" he cried. "Why, together with the widow's pledge, plus the bonus and the goat, why..."

Suddenly he stopped talking, for out of the bamboo thicket emerged a huge tiger followed by a cub. The older monk quickly drew his bow and shot off several arrows. Not one hit his target. The tigers advanced a step.

45

The second monk had only the heavy sheaf of temple records from which he had been reading. He threw the bundle with all his might at the tigers. The sheets scattered in a rain of fluttering white and black. To the monks' surprise, the tigers shied away from the paper and retreated into the thicket.

Puzzled but thankful, the monks hurried on their way.

In the bamboo thicket, the tiger cub looked curiously at his mother. "Why did you run, Mama? It was only paper."

His mother snarled. "I can fight thieves and robbers any day. And bows and arrows are nothing to me. But I cannot fight a monk who asks me for that many donations!"

Not surprisingly this story is a favorite with villagers who each year have to dig into their pockets for their temple's keep.

The Dragon Slayer

Chu was ambitious. He dreamed of the great things he would do someday. Everyone in the village expected him to be a success.

"Why don't you study with Master Kung?" his parents urged. "He is an excellent teacher!"

"There's no future in books," Chu replied.

His uncle, a wealthy farmer, advised him to take up the plow. "Farming is honest work. People must eat, so there's always a need to fill and money to be made."

"Too old-fashioned," Chu said disdainfully. "And too much dirt and sweat."

His father's friends urged him to master a craft, a technique, a skill of some kind—blacksmithing, pottery making, leather working, knife grinding.

Chu would have none of it. "A skilled man wastes his whole life crafting things for others," he objected. "He doesn't advance his own interest. That's not for me!"

His parents despaired their only son would have no goal in life. But one day, in the market, Chu heard of a man who roamed the hills for dragons to kill.

"Dragon slayer!" Chu's eyes gleamed. "Now that's my destiny!"

Chu gave his parents no rest until they agreed to let him enter an apprenticeship with a dragon slayer. Chu went to the city to begin training. His parents were reduced to near beggary to support his education.

Chu studied many books about the anatomy of dragons: the parts most heavily armored and resistant to attack by sword or spear, the parts most vulnerable. He learned their habits: where they dwelt, what they ate, when they roamed or slept. Most interesting of all, he immersed himself in the legendry and mythology of dragons. The stories filled him with awe and admiration for these fabulous creatures; at the same time they fed his ambition to become the most famous dragon slayer of all time. And all the while he studied from books, he practiced swordsmanship night and day and polished his skill with spear and battle-ax.

Finally, after three years, Chu returned home, eager to put his skills to use. He walked every mountain and valley of his province and the next, and the next after that, watched every pit and cave, and spent sleepless nights with herds of cows and sheep waiting for a dragon to swoop down for a meal.

Sadly, Chu found no dragons, and he was left with nothing to do.

48

鄭樂琳貳⊙壹壹

49

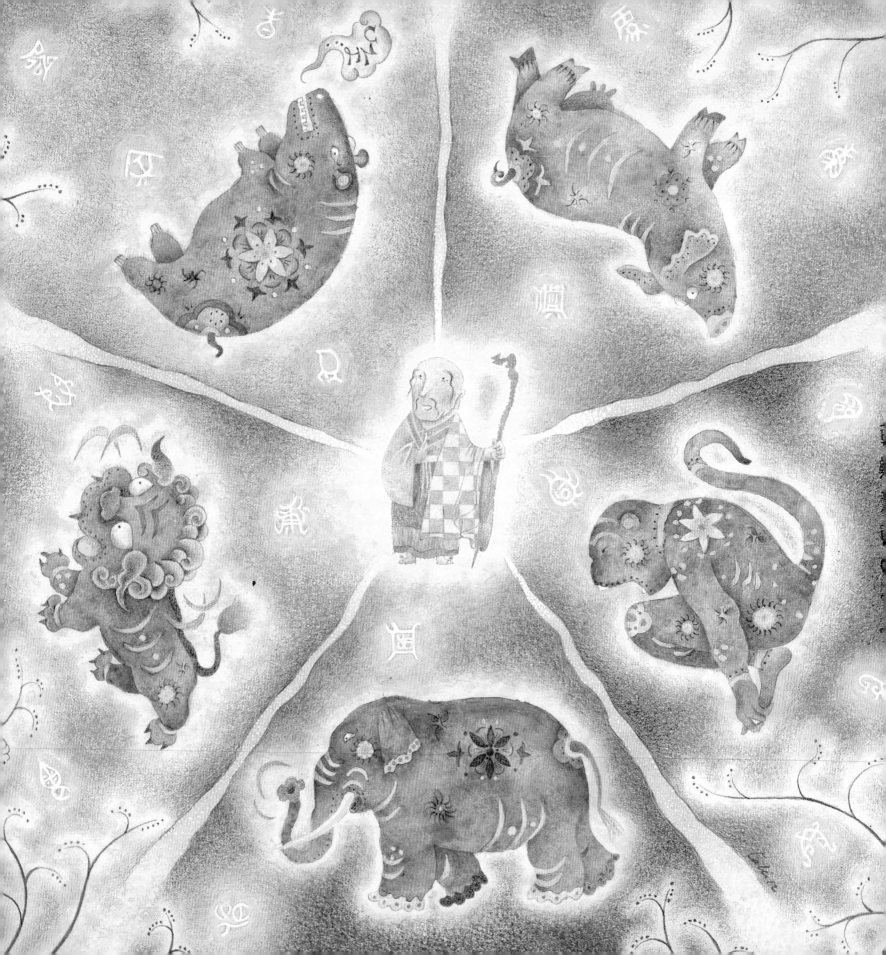

No Takers

Once a saint gazed upon earth's creatures and was saddened that all were burdened by at least one ugly feature.

"Elephant does not need all that nose," he said to himself. "It must get in his way. Monkey's mouth is way too wide for her little face. Small wonder she is inclined to senseless chatter and constant nibbling. And that long face of Horse! What could look more doleful?"

From forest to pasture to barn, the saint surveyed the animals to find one pleasing face, but in the end found none. Always one feature spoiled how they looked. Did Rhinoceros need that ugly horn on his nose? And Lion that frowsy mane like a tangled mop around his head? Look at how the oversized muzzle of Hippopotamus sagged! And Pig's snout, if not as offensive as Elephant's, was still a disgusting feature always buried in swill!

Moved with pity, the saint gathered the animals around him and said, "I will give you each a gift. I will change any face so that it will be pleasing to look upon. You have only to ask me, and it will be done."

Elephant curled his nose in the air and looked at Lion, who tossed his mane and eyed Hippopotamus, who grunted and aimed his muzzle at Pig. Monkey yawned, nearly splitting her little face in two.

There were no takers.

The Egg

A poor farmer, trudging home after a long day's labor in his landlord's field, found an egg on the road. Delighted, he picked it up, and all the rest of the way, he dreamed of the great change in fortune his lucky find would bring.

"Wife!" he announced as he stooped to enter their small hut. "We now have property!"

The farmer's wife was a woman of practical nature. "What property?" she scolded.

"Here." The farmer held out his hand, the egg cradled in his palm.

She hooted in laughter. "Just the thing to scramble in our soup tonight!" She reached for the egg, but her husband was quicker, and the egg was safe behind him.

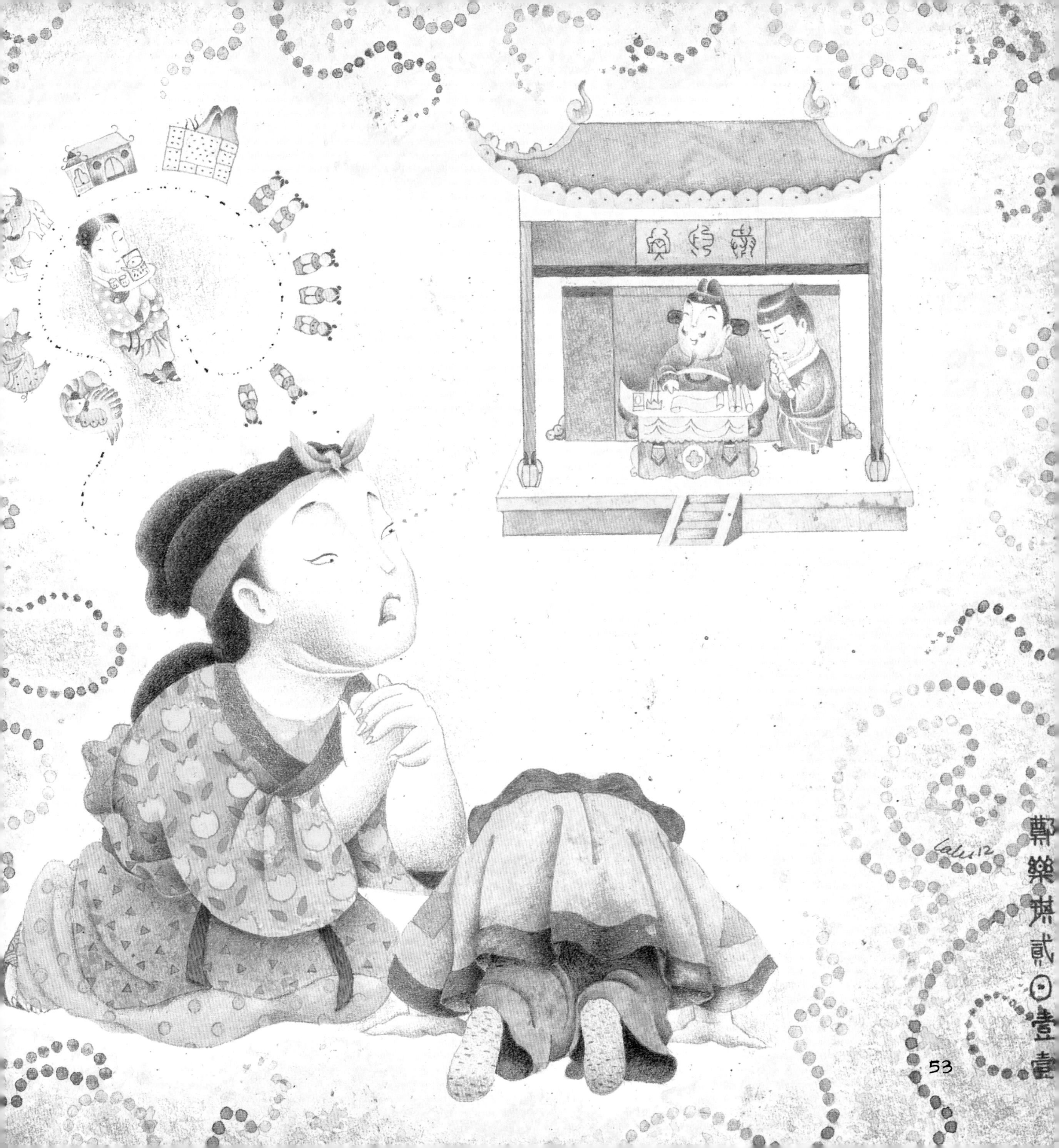
鄭樂琪貳〇壹壹

"Listen, Wife," he said, "this egg is our start. Tomorrow I will borrow a hen from Li to sit on the egg until it hatches. The chicken will lay more eggs, and we'll have more chicks and more eggs. When we sell the chickens, we can buy a small pig. A full-grown pig butchered for market can bring in enough to buy a calf. And when that calf is full- grown, we will sell it. Wife, what do you think we can do with all that money?"

"What can we do, Husband?" she asked. The practical wife's dormant imagination was slowly beginning to waken.

"We will lend that money and charge high interest!" The farmer's eyes sparkled. "Just think, Wife, in ten years we'll have enough to buy a house, a farm, servants—why, even a maid!"

"You're going to use our money to buy a maid?" Outraged, the wife darted forward, seized the egg, and threw it against the wall, where it dribbled to the floor.

The farmer took his wife to court for the malicious destruction of his property. When he told the judge of his ruined plans, the judge laughed heartily. Turning to the farmer's wife, he asked, "All these plans were in the future and indefinite. Why, were you already jealous?"

"His intentions are bad!" the practical wife declared. "Buy a maid indeed! I was only preventing such a thing from happening!"

鄭樂琪貳○壹壹

Welcome Guests

Master Ai-tse lived for three years in Ch'I as the guest of its ruler, the famous Lord Meng-ch'ang chün. When he returned home, the lord of his small province invited him to talk about his experiences.

"Tell me of Ch'i," his Lordship said. "Are all those stories we hear of its wonders true? They are hardly believable!"

So Ai-tse discoursed at length on the wonders of Ch'i, an enlightened society far in advance of its time.

His Lordship interrupted with the question he had most wanted to ask: "Is Meng-ch'ang Chün as great a ruler as everyone says? Does he deserve his reputation?"

Everything people say about him is true," Ai-tse replied, spreading out his arms. "Above all, he cannot be surpassed for his generosity of spirit."

"Oh?" his lordship said. "And how is that?"

"For one, his decisions are broad, never petty. He listens to all points of view."

"As I do," his Lordship nodded.

"And for another," Ai-tse went on, "he supports a thousand guests who come and go and keep his table lively with the most intelligent conversation."

"Enough!" his Lordship cut in testily. "No more praise of Meng-ch'an chün! I too am such a man to support many intelligent guests at my table! Drop by anytime and see!"

Some days later, Master Ai-tse dropped by his Lordship's, hoping to partake of duck and some exciting conversation. He found the hall empty except for his lordship seated alone, finishing a dish of noodles.

"Where are your guests?" Ai-tse asked.

"You are late, Sir; you missed the lively talk," his Lordship scolded. "My guests have gone home to eat their dinner!"

A Change of Fashion

The Lord Hsuan-Kung of Ch'i fell in love with the color red. He took to wearing a red coat with every change of costume. Never mind that his robe was peacock blue or pansy purple or jade green, he topped it off with a coat of red damask or red brocade. Always he wore red shoes to match.

Before long Hsuan-Kung noticed that every courtier was also wearing red. When he looked down from his dais on any assemblage of his court, he beheld a sea of red in its very shade and variation—carmine, scarlet, ruby, carnelian, vermilion, cerise, crimson, magenta.

Not one courtier was daring enough to wear a color that would be conspicuously different in that sea of red. The Lord Hsuan-Kung smiled benignly—how he loved red!

But it was not long before reports reached him of grumbling and unrest among the members of his court and the merchants of his city.

鄭樂琪貳○壹壹

"What are they saying?" he inquired of his spies.

"The complaints are many," reported the spy, drawing a sheaf of papers from the sleeve of his red cloak. "The merchants grumble that they can't make a profit on goods they don't have, or on goods they have but can't sell. They're out of red silk; there's a surplus of white silk because the dyers are out of red dye. The warehouses are full of silk in other colors, but nobody will buy it. Sire, your merchants are unhappy!"

"And my court—what is it saying?"

"Ah, your courtiers are just as unhappy." The spy pulled out another sheaf of papers from his sleeve. "Red overpowers personality, they say.

It diminishes the wearer, turns the complexion sallow. It becomes boring. Lady Jasmine hates it and threatens to leave her husband. Your courtiers wonder how you can be so blind to the glories of...purple...gold...saffron!"

The next morning the Lord Hsuan-Kung made his appearance at court in a white silk coat. He was as delighted over the astonished gasps that met him as he had been over the cries of praise for every new red coat.

The next day not a red coat was to be seen. In the whole of the city it is a matter of record that the shops had a run on white silk that week, followed in quick succession by runs on yellow, blue, green, and lavender.

Lak-Khee Tay-Audouard's whimsical illustrations are inspired by Chinese folk art. At the same time, basic elements of traditional Chinese art have been incorporated. Natural materials like earth, charcoal, ground tea powder, pressed leaves and sackcloth have been used to better portray the rustic quality of these tales. These pencil and wash illustrations were done on bamboo rag paper.

Published by Tuttle Publishing, an imprint of Periplus Editions (HK) Ltd.

www.tuttlepublishing.com

Copyright©2013 by Shiho S. Nunes
Illustrations©2013 Lak-Khee
Tay-Audouard

Library of Congress Cataloging-in-Publication Data

Nunes, Shiho S., 1917-
  Chinese fables : the dragon slayer and other timeless tales of wisdom / by Shiho S. Nunes ; illustrated by Lak-Khee Tay-Audouard.
      v. cm.
    ISBN 978-0-8048-4152-8 (hardback)
1. Fables, Chinese--Translations into English. 2. Tales--China. [1. Fables. 2. Folklore--China.] I. Tay-Audouard, L. K., ill. II. Title.
  PZ8.2.N96 Chi 2013
  398.2--dc23
  [E]

2012029059

ISBN 978-0-8048-4152-8

Distributed by

North America, Latin America Europe
Tuttle Publishing
364 Innovation Drive
North Clarendon,
VT 05759-9436 U.S.A.
Tel: 1 (802) 773-8930
Fax: 1 (802) 773-6993
info@tuttlepublishing.com
www.tuttlepublishing.com

Japan
Tuttle Publishing
Yaekari Building, 3rd Floor
5-4-12 Osaki
Shinagawa-ku
Tokyo 141 0032
Tel: (81) 3 5437-0171
Fax: (81) 3 5437-0755
sales@tuttle.co.jp
www.tuttle.co.jp

Asia Pacific
Berkeley Books Pte. Ltd.
61 Tai Seng Avenue #02-12
Singapore 534167
Tel: (65) 6280-1330
Fax: (65) 6280-6290
inquiries@periplus.com.sg
www.periplus.com

16 15 14 13
10 9 8 7 6 5 4 3 2 1

Printed in Malaysia   1211 TW
TUTTLE PUBLISHING® is a registered trademark of Tuttle Publishing, a division of Periplus Editions (HK) Ltd.

The Tuttle Story: "Books to Span the East and West"

Most people are surprised to learn that the world's largest publisher of books on Asia had its humble beginnings in the tiny American state of Vermont. The company's founder, Charles E. Tuttle, belonged to a New England family steeped in publishing. And his first love was naturally books—especially old and rare editions.

Immediately after WW II, serving in Tokyo under General Douglas MacArthur, Tuttle was tasked with reviving the Japanese publishing industry. He later founded the Charles E. Tuttle Publishing Company, which thrives today as one of the world's leading independent publishers.

Though a westerner, Tuttle was hugely instrumental in bringing a knowledge of Japan and Asia to a world hungry for information about the East. By the time of his death in 1993, Tuttle had published over 6,000 books on Asian culture, history and art—a legacy honored by the Japanese emperor with the "Order of the Sacred Treasure," the highest tribute Japan can bestow upon a non-Japanese.

With a backlist of 1,500 titles, Tuttle Publishing is more active today than at any time in its past—inspired by Charles Tuttle's core mission to publish fine books to span the East and West and provide a greater understanding of each.